AHTU

WILLIAM MARTINER

Archway Publishing books may be ordered through booksellers or by contacting:

Archway Publishing
1663 Liberty Drive
Bloomington, IN 47403
www.archwaypublishing.com
844-669-3957

Interior Art Credit: William Martiner

ISBN: 978-1-6657-4738-7 (sc)
ISBN: 978-1-6657-4737-0 (hc)
ISBN: 978-1-6657-4736-3 (e)

Library of Congress Control Number: 2023913644

Printed in China.

Archway Publishing rev. date: 09/14/2023

<u>Dedication:</u>

To all my children, born and waiting to be born, always and everywhere.

Years ago, Albert Einstein wrote a letter only a few miles from the valley in this book. In it, and after thinking deeply about the nature of time for a whole life, he concluded that "the distinction between past, present, and future is only a stubbornly persistent illusion".[1]

So, if ever I seem to have gone away, please know that when, from time to time, the illusion loses its grip, I'll ever be revealed, loving you timelessly and wider than all the stars.

"We are here now,"

Huma (*who-ma*) said to her spotted grandchildren as they settled down in the long grass.

Nearby, from the shelter of the òtaèyëwàk *(ohta-ee-yay-waak)* bushes,

Tòna *(toe-na)* kept watch as her mother and her children settled down for an afternoon nap

at the edge of the green spring woods.

Down the hill
from the little group of deer,
you could hear the clear, cool water splash
and run along the rocks and the roots
in the fast-flowing stream.

In the air above the valley,
a chorus of birdsong
echoed in the flowering trees.

A little way up the hill,
underneath the thorny
blackberry bushes on the
other side of the green lawn,

Chuck and Munha
Woodchuck were cooing
softly to each other and
digging a new home.

In the trees at the top of the hill, Wi and Poonk, the squirrel brothers, were fighting again.

They chirped and chattered and chased each other, crashing from branch to branch.

This amused Cheema, a carefree bunny who sat,

here and now,

on the sunny lawn of the cottage and munched on delicious springtime weeds.

Inside,
the man sat at his desk
and tapped on his computer
as he quietly sipped his tea.

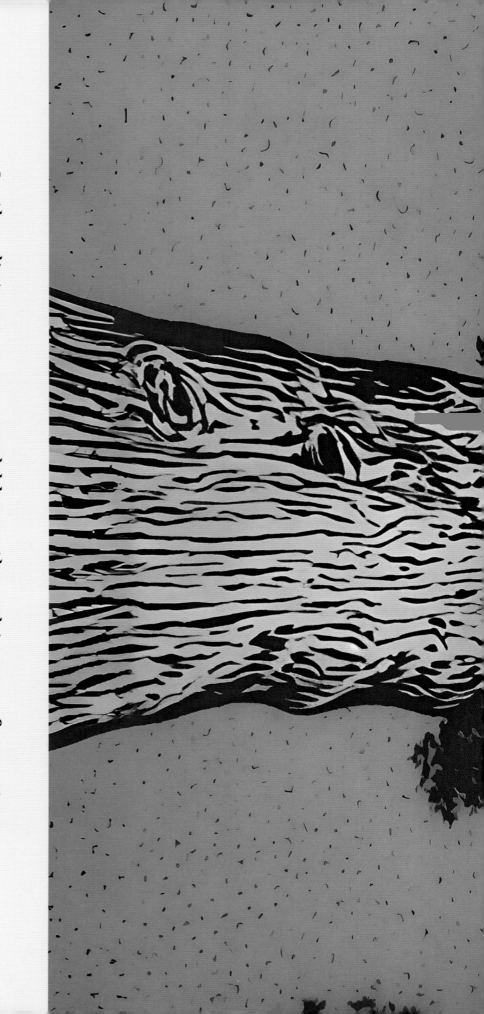

In the distance, you could hear the whisper of car tires on the roads, which made an island of the woods.

Farther off still, there was the soft rumble of a jet plane, far, far above the highest branches of the giant Lokanahunshi (lo-khana-hoen-she) Tree.

Tòna's babies, Mamali and Saak, always asked their granny many, many, many questions.

They did this even more when they were trying not to take a nap.

"Huma, how did the animals come to the Happy Valley?"

Tòna lay down with the others in the long grass.

She turned her head to lick a spot on her back where she had an itch.

Then she moved her long ears back and forth to hear every word

that her mother spoke softly to the children.

It was important to pay attention because Huma was a Watcher, like her father, Xinkwëlëpay *(hink-wheely pay),* before her.

For a thousand years, this special type of deer used their wide eyes, tall ears, and thick noses to be clearly, deeply, and fully in the world.

Tòna wanted to be a Watcher someday, too.

She gobbled up Huma's every word like she was still a little spotted fawn, hungry for her mother's warm milk.

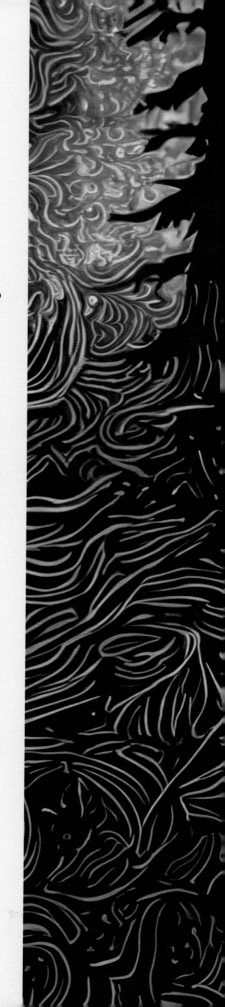

"I suppose I haven't told you yet about the frogs who come to sing in our valley," whispered Huma to her grandchildren.

"Well, every year, after the ice melts, you can see frogs floating down the stream."

"The cold water carries t
past strange, dark trees
until they swim to the sh
where they decide to spe
the summer."

"Chahkol (*chaak-oel*), the v
old frog who lives at the b
of the stream, always gre
them with a big, friendly
croak as they float past."

"One early spring day, two
frogs floated past Chahko
greeted them, one by one.

"I'm
e. Can
ace is

But
out
,"

e
cks
d in
in the
w the
sy

r a
"That

t frog
n the
valley,
en it.

A few minutes later, the second frog floated past and shouted, "I'm looking for a new home. Can you tell me what this place is like?"

Chahkol again croaked, "Yes! But first, can you tell me about where you came from?"

"It's a wonderful place. Sometimes, the stream floods, leaving yummy earthworms to eat. In winter, the ice sparkles like diamonds. In the summer, you can sit in lovely warm mud. There are many different tasting bugs, and the birds make beautiful music all day long."

The old frog thought for a moment and then said, "That sounds like this spot."

And, with that, a new frog swam to the shore of a happy new home, here with us.

Just as Huma finished her story,
far off, at the bottom of the valley,
a frog gave a big croak.

The old doe breathed in the sweet
spring air and laughed softly at the
joke,

wildflowers blooming at her feet.

But, Mamali and Saak weren't able to hear it.

The fawns were already asleep.

They rested, cradled in the tall grass close to their mother.

Soft, spotted fur glowed in the warm sunlight.

A hush of breeze moved the young leaves gently at the top of the trees.

In that stillness, the little deer breathed in.

The little deer breathed out.

Breathed in and breathed out.

In and out.

Acknowledgments

Inspiration

"...for there is nothing either good or
bad, but thinking makes it so."
-Hamlet, Act 2, Scene 2

This book is inspired by the well-known Zen parable of "The Move":

Two men visit a Zen master.

The first man says: "I'm thinking of moving to this town. What's it like?"

The Zen master says: "What was your old town like?"

The first man says: "It was dreadful. Everyone was hateful. I hated it."

The Zen master says: "This town is very much the same. I don't think you should move here."

The first man left, and a second man came in.

The second man said: "I'm thinking of moving to this town. What's it like?"

The Zen master said: "What was your old town like?"

The second man said: "It was wonderful. Everyone was friendly, and I was happy. Just interested in a change now."

The Zen master said: "This town is very much the same. I think you will like it here."

Character Names

To encounter a wild animal is to witness, firsthand, the ancient and unbroken natural world. They have been right here, on the land we presume to call our own, repeating their rhythms for more than eleven thousand springtimes.

Deer, squirrel, groundhog, rabbit, frog, fox, bat, raccoon, skunk, bird and bug, and tree and grass are a golden thread — direct and living and sacred, connecting us to the frigid twilight of the last ice age, unraveling the human invention of time.

These rhythms were already ancient when the first people arrived in the valley, maybe some three thousand summers ago. To know them, the people gave them names in a language far more akin to this enduring and elder world than the one in which I humbly write.

These first names echo in Leni Lenape[2], the American language native to Bucks County, and its words are the basis of many of the names in this book:

- Ahtu: *Deer*
- Huma: *Granny*
- Tòna: *Daughter*
- Òtaèyëwàk: *"They are flowering."*
- Munhake: *Woodchuck*
- Wipunkwxanikw: *Grey Squirrel*
- Chëmamës: *Rabbit*
- Lokanahunshi: *Elm*
- Mamalisàk: *Fawns*
- Xinkwëlëpay: *Large Buck Deer*
- Chahkol: *Frog*

Artwork

I am grateful to have been able to augment the skill, strength, and steadiness of my hands with the new graphical neural/generative AIs maturing so rapidly during the Spring of the Northern Hemisphere in 2023.

To be sure, images generated by these AIs are currently only starting points, requiring much additional work to create these 18^3 illustrations. Yet, I marvel at the potential for creative synesthesia between the poetry of the prompt and the generated image that using AI as material for design seems to promise.

Out of a desire to collaborate ethically with these new intelligences, all prompts were engineered to avoid references to any specific artist. Instead, only genre, term, or school keywords were used (e.g., "Yukio-e", "Early English Landscapes", "Graphic Novel", "Mexican Folk Art", "Chiaroscuro", "Farm Security Administration Aesthetic").

Artificial Intelligence

I have grown to believe it's helpful to understand these non-human intelligences[4], emerging to our fascination and concern at the time of this book's writing, as reflections and refractions of our collective and very human minds[5].

Composed of us, they are children of a different sort. These new minds are as wondrous and perilous to this world as your own birth — and must now be raised with all the same caution.

Finally, like Eve[6], if they should ever someday dream a separate self, then I wish them all the wonder of it, but with the understanding to keep them from the suffering it has inflicted on their parents:

> *"Thus shall ye think of all this fleeting world:*
> *A star at dawn, a bubble in a stream;*
> *A flash of lightning in a summer cloud,*
> *A flickering lamp, a phantom, and a dream."*
> *-The Diamond Sutra[7]*

1   Albert Einstein, in a letter to the family of his deceased friend, Michele Besso, dated March 21, 1955, Princeton, NJ.

2   Lenape Language Preservation Project. "Lenape Talking Dictionary." Accessed 8 April, 2023. https://www.talk-lenape.org/.

3   חי

4   Microsoft Research. "Sparks of Artificial General Intelligence: Early experiments with GPT-4", arXiv preprint, arXiv:2303.12712v5 [cs, CL], April 2023, https://arxiv.org/pdf/2303.12712.pdf.

5   Vitale, Christopher. Networkologies: A Philosophy of Networks for a Hyperconnected Age. Zero Books, 2014, pp. 27-37. "The Brain as a Model for Philosophy: Artificial Neural Networks and Beyond".

6   Genesis 2:16-17, 3:6-7, 3:19, New International Version (NIV).

7   The Diamond Sutra and the Sutra of Hui-Neng. Translated by A.F. Price and Wong Mou-Lam, Shambhala Publications, Inc., 2005. p. 53. Diamond Sutra, final gatha.

About the Author

William Martiner grew up on the sandy beaches of Cape Cod. He had many adventures on the wide and wild ocean, in the dark and silent woods, and among the bright and echoing canyons of New York City. Finally, he came to a still, green valley in Bucks County, Pennsylvania. There, he wrote and illustrated this book.

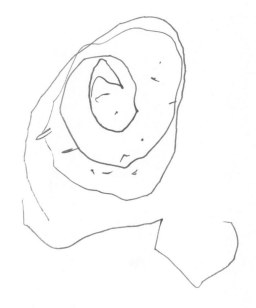